OLIVIA

and the

Fairy Princesses

written and illustrated by Ian Falconer

Atheneum
ATHENEUM BOOKS FOR YOUNG READERS
New York   London   Toronto   Sydney   New Delhi

With deepest apologies to Martha Graham

ATHENEUM BOOKS FOR YOUNG READERS
An imprint of Simon & Schuster Children's Publishing Division
1230 Avenue of the Americas, New York, New York 10020
Copyright © 2012 by Ian Falconer
Photograph on pages 26, 29, and 35 is of Martha Graham, *Lamentations* (oblique), 1935 / © Barbara Morgan, The Barbara Morgan Archive
Photograph on page 33 is of *Foyer of the Opera, Paris* / © Michael Maslan Historic Photographs/CORBIS
ATHENEUM BOOKS FOR YOUNG READERS is a registered trademark of Simon & Schuster, Inc.
Atheneum logo is a trademark of Simon & Schuster, Inc.
For information about special discounts for bulk purchases, please contact Simon & Schuster Special Sales at 1-866-506-1949 or business@simonandschuster.com.
The Simon & Schuster Speakers Bureau can bring authors to your live event. For more information or to book an event, contact the Simon & Schuster Speakers Bureau at 1-866-248-3049 or visit our website at www.simonspeakers.com.
Book design by Ann Bobco
The text for this book is set in Centaur MT.
The illustrations for this book are rendered in charcoal and gouache on paper.
Manufactured in China
0612 SCP
First Edition
10 9 8 7 6 5 4 3 2 1
Library of Congress Cataloging-in-Publication Data
Falconer, Ian, 1959–
Olivia and the fairy princesses / Ian Falconer. — 1st ed.
p. cm.
Summary: "Olivia is having an identity crisis! There are too many ruffly, sparkly princesses around these days, and Olivia has had quite enough. She needs to stand out! She has to be special! What will she be? Join Olivia on a hilarious quest for individuality in this latest book of the Olivia series, and rest assured, you won't find THIS pig in pink!"—Provided by publisher.
ISBN 978-1-4424-5027-1 (hardcover)
ISBN 978-1-4424-5028-8 (eBook)
[1. Individuality—Fiction. 2. Princesses—Fiction. 3. Pigs—Fiction.]
I. Title.
PZ7.F1865Old 2012
[E]—dc23   2011053046

Olivia was depressed.

"I think I'm having
an identity crisis,"
she told her parents.

"I don't know what I should be!"

"Well," said her father, "you'll always be my little princess!"

"That's the problem," said Olivia. "All the girls want to be princesses.

"At Pippa's birthday party, they were all dressed in big, pink, ruffly skirts with sparkles and little crowns and sparkly wands. Including some of the boys.

"I chose a simple French sailor shirt, matador pants, black flats, a strand of pearls, sunglasses, a red bag, and my gardening hat.

"Why is it always a pink princess? Why not an Indian princess or a princess from Thailand or an African princess or a princess from China?

"There *are* alternatives.

"For the school dance recital, *everyone* was trying out for the fairy princess ballerina. Even a couple of the boys."

"But, Olivia," said her mother,
"I seem to remember last year
you wanting to be a ballerina."

"That was when I was little.

"I'm trying to develop a more stark, modern style."

"Olivia, it's time for your bath," said her mother.

"And on Halloween,"
said Olivia, "what did
all the girls go as?"

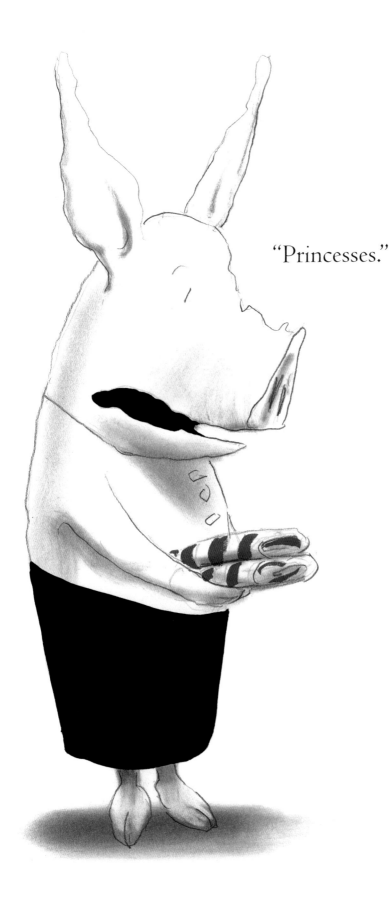

"Princesses."

"Princesses!"

"I went
as a
warthog.

It was
very
effective.

"If everyone's a princess, then princesses aren't special anymore!" said Olivia.

"Why do they
all want to be
the same?"

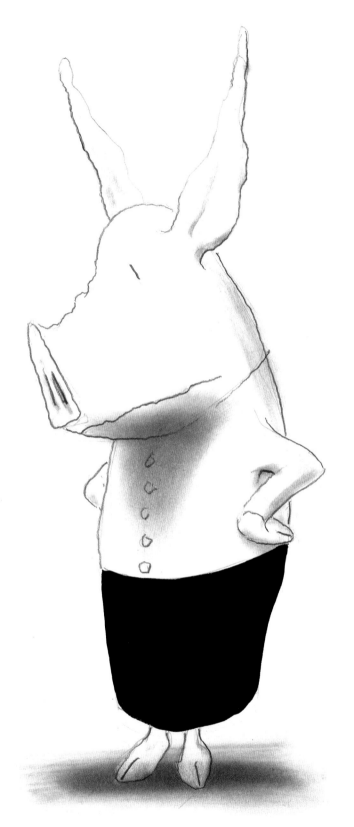

After her bath, Olivia's mother read her a story. It was about a beautiful maiden who was locked in a tower by an evil queen.

"'When a prince came along, rescued her, and made her his—'"

"Not his princess!" cried Olivia.

"Fine," said her mother, who was tiring of this discussion. "I'll read you the story of the Little Match Girl. 'Once there was a little girl who was forced to sell matches barefoot in the snow.

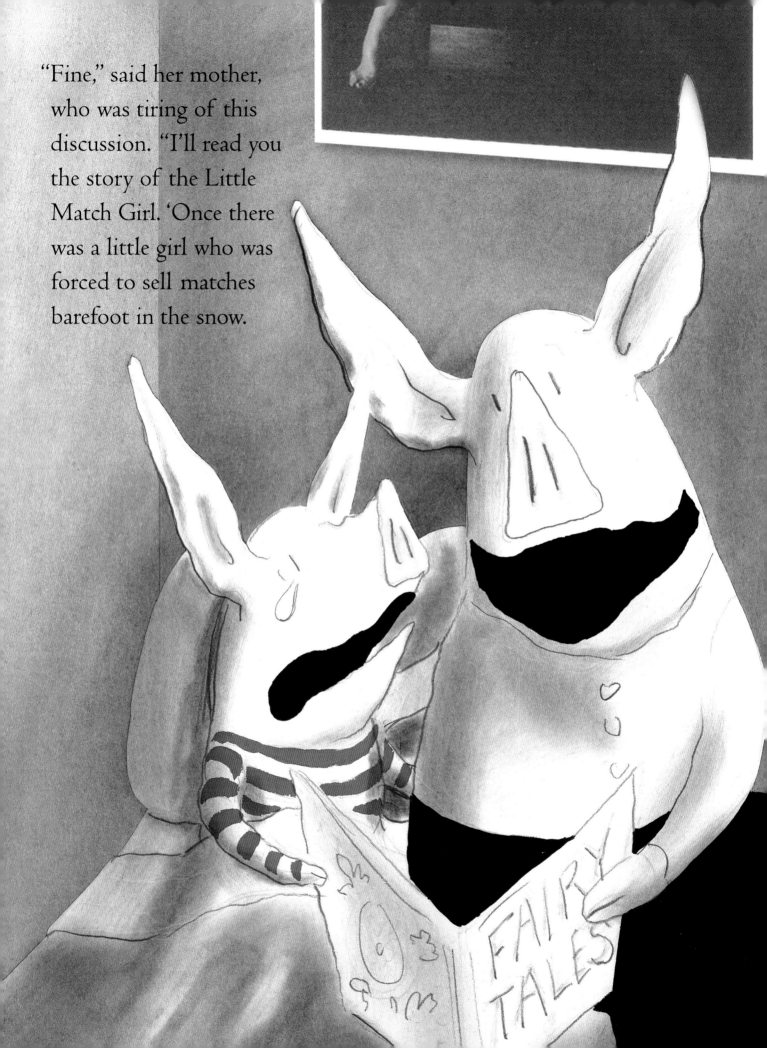

"'The matches kept her warm for a while, but all too soon they ran out. . . .'"

"Oh, Mommy, that's so sad," said Olivia, tearing up. "I may not want to be a princess, but I wouldn't want to be freezing in the snow."

Her mother said, "Well, I want you to be ASLEEP in five minutes!"

"But first read me the story about Little Red Riding Hood!"

"No, Olivia, it's bedtime."

"Just the parts where everyone gets eaten. Please?"

"No. I'm turning out the light."

Olivia lay in the dark trying to sleep,
but her brain wouldn't let her.

"Maybe I could be a nurse and devote myself
to the sick and the elderly.

"I could use my brothers to practice bandaging.

"And various other treatments.

"Or maybe adopt orphans from all over the world!

"Or I could be a reporter and expose corporate malfeasance."

Hmm . . .

Then it occurred to her.
"I know . . .

"I want to be queen."